Dear Parents and Educators,

Welcome to Penguin Young Readers! As parents and educators, you know that each child develops at his or her own pace—in terms of speech, critical thinking, and, of course, reading. Penguin Young Readers recognizes this fact. As a result, each Penguin Young Readers book is assigned a traditional easy-to-read level (1–4) as well as an F&P Text Level (A–P). Both of these systems will help you choose the right book for your child. Please refer to the back of each book for specific leveling information. Penguin Young Readers features esteemed authors and illustrators, stories about favorite characters, fascinating nonfiction, and more!

Mr. Men Little Miss: Pirate Adventure

LEVEL 3

F&P TEXT
LEVEL **J**

This book is perfect for a **Transitional Reader** who:
- can read multisyllable and compound words;
- can read words with prefixes and suffixes;
- is able to identify story elements (beginning, middle, end, plot, setting, characters, problem, solution); and
- can understand different points of view.

Here are some **activities** you can do during and after reading this book:
- Reading with Expression: Although many transitional readers can read text accurately, they may read slowly or not smoothly, and pay little or no attention to punctuation. One way to improve this is to read out loud with the child. For example, read page 24 in this story out loud. Ask the child to pay attention to how your voice changes when you come to different punctuation marks, such as the exclamation point, period, and question mark. Then have the child read another page out loud to you.
- Character Traits: In this story, many of the characters have names that describe their traits. Can you name some of them? How would you describe Captain Yellowbeard and the pirates?

Remember, sharing the love of reading with a child is the best gift you can give!

D0594952

*This book has been officially leveled by using the F&P Text Level Gradient™ leveling system.

PENGUIN YOUNG READERS

An Imprint of Penguin Random House LLC, New York

Adapted from *Mr. Men Adventure with Pirates*. Published by
Penguin Young Readers, an imprint of Penguin Random House LLC, New York.
Manufactured in China.

www.mrmen.com

Visit us online at www.penguinrandomhouse.com.

ISBN 9781524792398 (pbk)   10 9 8 7 6 5 4 3 2 1
ISBN 9781524792558 (hc)   10 9 8 7 6 5 4 3 2 1

PENGUIN YOUNG READERS

LEVEL 3

TRANSITIONAL READER

MR. MEN LITTLE MISS

PIRATE ADVENTURE

originated by Roger Hargreaves

adapted by Lana Edelman

illustrated by Adam Hargreaves

Mr. Happy and his friends
are happy.

They are sailing on a boat.

Mr. Happy is the captain.

Look!
A big ship
is coming
toward them.

Oh no.

The people on the ship

do not look nice.

It is a pirate ship!

Yellowbeard is the captain.

Yellowbeard gives everyone

a choice.

They can become a pirate or

walk the plank.

Everyone chooses to become

a pirate.

Everyone except Mr. Impossible.

He chooses to walk the plank.

Oh no!

Mr. Impossible will fall into the water if he walks the plank.

There are sharks in the water!

Look!

Mr. Impossible does not fall into
the water.

He walks in the air.

His feet do not even get wet!

Mr. Lazy thinks being on the ship

is hard work.

He has to wake up early.

That is not easy for Mr. Lazy.

Mr. Dizzy thinks being on the
ship is hard work, too.

Everyone wants eggs.

But it is hard to cook on a ship
that is moving!

Of course, Mr. Wrong gets

his job wrong.

Look out!

Mr. Wrong shoots the cannon

in the wrong direction.

Yellowbeard has a big job for

Mr. Happy and his friends.

He wants them to find

a buried treasure.

The treasure is on a ship

at the bottom of the ocean.

Yellowbeard and his pirates

cannot swim.

Mr. Wrong has a big job.

He has to find a secret island

with his looking glass.

That is where the sunken

ship is.

He uses the wrong end of

the looking glass.

How will he ever find the

secret island?

Silly Mr. Wrong!

Mr. Happy goes underwater
to find the treasure.
He wears a special diving suit.

Look out!

There are sharks swimming
around the treasure.
How will Mr. Happy get
to the treasure?

Mr. Impossible can help!

He turns the water from

blue to pink.

How did he do that?

The pink water surprises

the sharks.

The sharks swim away!

Uh-oh!

There is a big octopus on top of

the treasure.

How will they get the

treasure now?

Mr. Tickle can help!

Mr. Forgetful has a big job.

He must bury the treasure to

keep it safe.

He digs a big hole and

puts the chest into the hole.

Then he wakes up

Captain Yellowbeard.

Oh no!

Mr. Forgetful forgets where

he buried the treasure.

Yellowbeard is mad.

Mr. Happy and his friends steal
a boat and paddle away from
Yellowbeard and his pirates.

The pirates are stuck on the
island now.

Mr. Happy and his friends are
happy again.

Mr. Happy is the captain of the
boat now.

Hooray for Mr. Happy!